© 1991 Comprehensive Health Education Foundation (*CHEF*®);
Roberts, Fitzmahan & Associates, Inc. (RF&A)
All rights reserved.
Printed in the United States of America.
95 94 93 92    10 9 8 7 6 5 4 3
8/92    20K

Library of Congress Cataloging-in-Publication Data
Starkman, Neal.
      The forever secret / by Neal Starkman; illustrated by G. Brian Karas.
      p.  cm.
      Summary: A fifth-grader relates the problems caused by an alcoholic parent.
      [1. Alcoholism--Fiction.  2. Family problems--Fiction.  3. II fa04 04-22-91.]
      I. Karas, G. Brian, ill.  II. Title.
      PZ7.S7955Fo  1991  [Fic]--dc20

ISBN 0-935529-28-4                                                                91-16799

The
FOR EVER
SECRET

# SECRET

I have a secret. I feel as if it fills up my brain and the top of my head's going to BLOW OFF.

But not only can't I tell anyone this secret, there's this, too:

I can't even tell anyone that I have a secret. That's the TOUGH part.

My dad and my brother Mark say, "No one must know. You must keep this secret forever. It's a family secret. Everything is just fine." But I don't believe it.

I'm going to write some of this down.

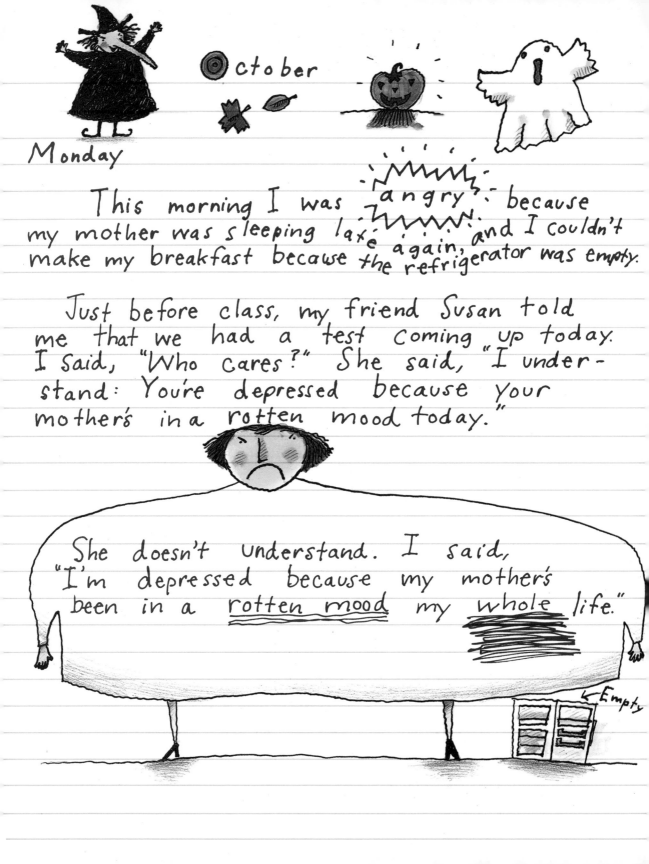

October

Monday

This morning I was **angry** because my mother was sleeping late again, and I couldn't make my breakfast because the refrigerator was empty.

Just before class, my friend Susan told me that we had a test coming up today. I said, "Who cares?" She said, "I understand: You're depressed because your mother's in a rotten mood today."

She doesn't understand. I said, "I'm depressed because my mother's been in a rotten mood my whole life."

← Empty

Wednesday:

Tonight the fighting is <u>BAD</u>!

I'm lying as close to the wall as I can, and I'm trying to write while listening to all the yelling and crying and cursing.
    So maybe this is all <u>my fault</u>. Maybe, somehow, I caused all this. Maybe my mother's right when she says, "You should <u>never</u> have been <u>born</u>!" or "You're the reason I drink!" I mean, it's possible. If I was different, or if I wasn't ~~here yet~~ here at all, then maybe things would get better. If <u>I</u> was better, then maybe things would get better.

<u>NO</u>! That doesn't make sense. But this yelling all the ~~time~~ doesn't make sense, either.

Thursday:

My brother Mark is five years older than me. This evening I started to talk to him about Mom, and he changed the subject so fast I didn't even realize it until we were in the middle of talking about pizza.

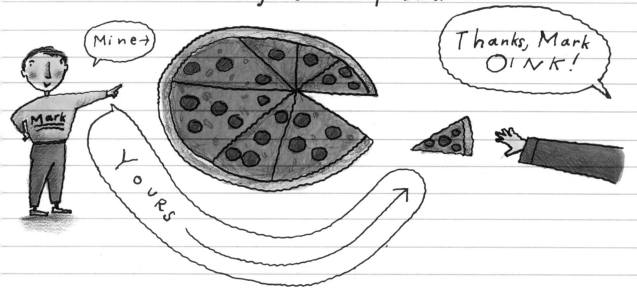

Mark doesn't want to talk about questions that don't have any answers. I'm different: I like questions that don't have any answers, because you can never be wrong.

<u>Saturday</u>

Here's what happened this morning:

10:25 - My mother is supposed to take me to my friend Wayne's birthday party; my father's working and I can't find Mark. The party's at 11:00 but my mother is in :<u>NO</u>: condition to drive. It's probably too late to call for a ride. I decide not to wrap Wayne's present, since I can give it to him on Monday.

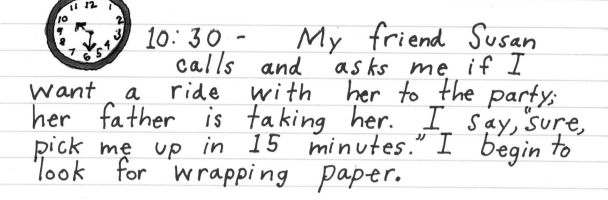

10:30 - My friend Susan calls and asks me if I want a ride with her to the party; her father is taking her. I say, "Sure, pick me up in 15 minutes." I begin to look for wrapping paper.

10:33 - My mother hears me talking to Susan and remembers the party. She offers to take me and Susan. I say, "No, Mom, that's OK, I have a ride." She says, "Nonsense, I'll take you both." I don't know what to do, and so I say, "I'm really feeling sick and I don't think I'll go at all," figuring that it's better not to go than to get into an accident on the way. I put away the wrapping paper.

10:35 - I call Susan, to say thanks, anyway, but I'm feeling sick and can't go. But Susan isn't there; they've already left. I frantically wrap the present as I try to think about what I'll tell my mother when Susan gets here.

10:38 - My mother tells me that it's just as well I'm not feeling well because she's not feeling very well, either, and she doesn't like driving when she feels like this. Then she frowns and asks me why I'm wrapping a present, and so quickly. I say I kind of feel better, it must have been the 24-minute flu or something. She says, "That's ~~the~~ 24-HOUR flu."

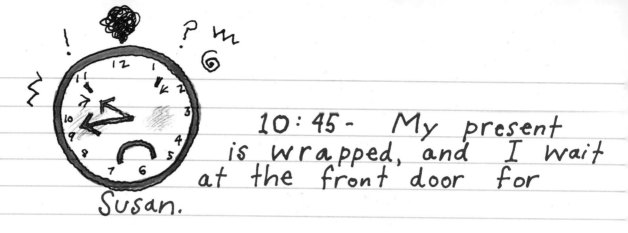

10:45 - My present is wrapped, and I wait at the front door for Susan.

10:55 - Susan calls. The car broke down. Can I find another way to get there?

10:56 - I decide that birthday parties are sometimes too much trouble. I am absolutely certain that NO other family in the WORLD has to go through stuff like this.

Mom sick in bed    +

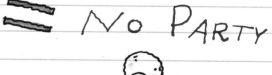

= NO PARTY

## Tuesday

Here's a flash: Alcoholism is a <u>disease</u>! That's what we learned in school today. Strange disease. I don't get punished when my brother gets chicken pox. I don't get punished when my father gets a cold. But I get punished because my mother has <u>alcoholism</u>. What do I care what alcoholism is? I know what it <u>does</u>.

There once was a mom,
who usually was calm,
until she drank lots of booze;
Then the liquor inside her
turned her into a fighter,
but in this fight
everyone would lose.

I'll tell you one thing: I refuse to become like my mother. If it means that I won't ever drink, then that's what it'll be.
NOTHING can be worse than

acting like my mother.

# BAD

This evening my mother said to me, "You're just <u>no good</u>! You'll never amount to <u>anything</u>!"

Okay, she's told me that before. Big deal. But this time my father was right there when she said it. At least he could have defended me.

Mark is nice to me tonight, asks me if I want to go shopping to get some new tennis shoes.

He wants me to say yes so he can feel that I'm okay. I want new tennis shoes, but I don't want Mark to feel that I can just forget the things Mom says to me. I say, "Some other time."

# Wednesday

    <u>Wanted</u>: a new family. Must have a mother who doesn't drink, doesn't yell, doesn't break promises, doesn't say awful things, doesn't embarrass you. Must have a father who sticks up for you. Brother not necessary.

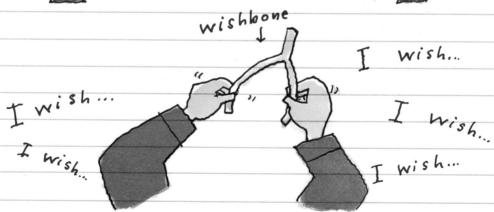

wishbone ↓

I wish...

I wish...

I wish...

I wish...

I wish...

<u>Sunday</u>

Susan came over to my house today without calling, and she saw my mother drunk. I was <u>really</u> <u>angry</u> with her—

Susan, that is. Mom couldn't help herself, but Susan should have called. I yelled at her, and she left fast. I figured I'd call her up tonight, but I really didn't ever want to see her again.

So I called her and we talked awhile. <u>She</u> talked, anyway. I couldn't say much except no and uh-huh, because someone might have been listening. She said she understood and I said uh-huh. She said it must be

real bad for me, and I said uh-huh. Then she suggested that I talk with the school nurse about it. She said, "You like Mrs. Nay.

Remember, you always used to hang out there last year. You said she was like a second mother."
     Actually, what I said was, she, was like a <u>first</u> mother. But I'm not so sure I can talk to Mrs. Nay about this.

## Wednesday

    I found out something that helps: I make out lists. I write all the different vegetables I can think of — "artichokes" for "a", "brussels sprouts" for "b," "carrots" for "c," and so on.

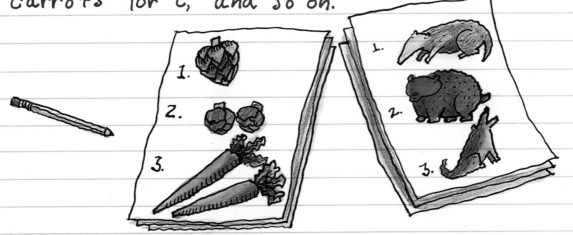

Or I write all the animals I can think of — "anteater" for "a", "bear" for "b", "coyote" for "c." Or I list all the states, or the presidents, or countries, or fruits, or TV shows, or anything. Along with loud music and stories about places far from here, it helps me not to think about what's going on around the house.

# Thursday

## 5 Things I Try to Think About My Mother

1. She does offensive things because she drinks.
2. She can't stop drinking.
3. She didn't start drinking because of me.
4. She won't stop drinking because of me.
5. She really loves me, or maybe likes me a lot. Okay, maybe she likes me enough.

## 5 Things About Myself

1. I like to make lists.
2. I like to make lists to take my mind off my mother.
3. Sometimes making lists doesn't always help me take my mind off my mother.
4. Sometimes I get so tired of making lists that I don't even finish them.

# Monday

Our class put on a play today, just a little one. I had the part of a doctor. It was great! Putting on plays is the best thing a class can do. I think I like acting because I can be someone else, even if it's for just a little while.

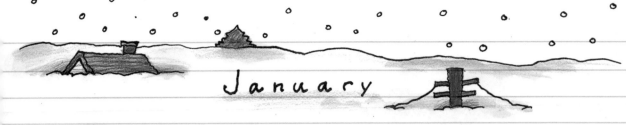

January

<u>Thursday</u>

I haven't written much lately. But here's a story:

## <u>A STORY ABOUT ME AND MY MOTHER</u>

Once upon a time, a few years ago, all the kids in my class were going to have their pictures taken, and we were supposed to wear something nice that day. When I went home and told my mother, she was sober and said, "Let's go shopping Tuesday evening and get you a new shirt and pair of shoes so you look nice for the pictures on Wednesday." On Tuesday, though, my mother got drunk. When my father came home from work there was a lot of hollering and crying, so we didn't go shopping. On Wednesday I was the only one not dressed up. My teacher wanted to know whether I forgot to dress up. I said yes, I forgot, and the class laughed.

## The End
(It's not made up.)

me

## Friday
I <u>never</u> want to become addicted to alcohol! It's really important for me to remember that.

## February

### Wednesday

Another Story — This one About How My Mother Started to Drink

My mother was young, and one of her friends asked her if she wanted to drink. She said, sure, one drink can't hurt. She didn't like it, but everyone else was drinking, so she did, too. She would drink to celebrate birthdays, to relax, and just because she felt like it.

Years later, when she got married and then had kids, she would drink to calm her nerves after a hard day. Pretty soon she would drink even if she didn't have a hard day. When she stopped drinking, she wasn't as happy as when she <u>was</u> drinking, so she continued to drink.

Then she got addicted, which means that she found it really hard to stop drinking even if she wanted to.

Then everybody got mad at her for drinking, and she got mad at everybody else. She said she didn't have a problem.

The End

<u>Tuesday</u>

| Monday | Tuesday | Wednesday | Thursday | Friday |
|--------|---------|-----------|----------|--------|
|        |         |           |          |        |

I guess I should write about this: I got into trouble today because I talked back to my teacher. Well, I yelled at her, actually. She just kept <u>bothering</u> me about this math problem. I told her I didn't know, but she wouldn't stop asking me. So I told her off. And she sent me to the office. And I stayed after school. Mark finally came for me, and promised to tell our parents that I got into trouble, but I know he won't. Mark will do anything to avoid a fight, and <u>boy</u>, would there be

<u>a fight</u>    if Mom and Dad knew   what I did today. We  have  enough fights already.
.  .  .  .  .  .  .

Every   time  I'm  emotional now, Susan thinks  it's  because of  my  mother. You know what's tough?  I   want  people  to know   that   I  have a problem, but I don't want them to treat  me  differently.   Like, Sometimes  I'm   sad  because I  had  a  fight  with  a  friend. Sometimes    I'm  angry because I heard   a   rumor  about  me. Sometimes   I'm  confused because  I   can't  figure  out what  my  homework  assignment is.  <u>Everything</u> <u>doesn't</u> revolve around  my  mother.

SAD      CONFUSED      ANGRY

## Wednesday

I'm not eating carrots anymore. I usually eat a carrot for lunch. Then today someone said, "You're addicted to those things, aren't you."

I am <u>NEVER</u> going to be addicted to anything. <u>N E V E R</u>

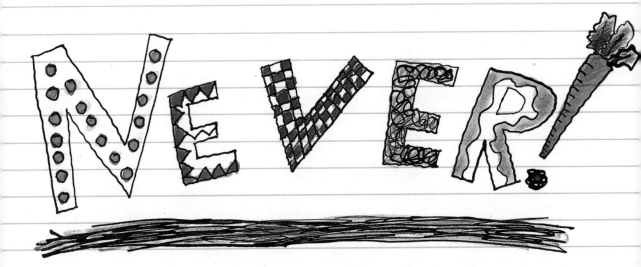

<u>Friday</u>

So I went to Mrs. Nay, the school nurse, and I told her about Mom, sort of. I mean, I started by asking her for ways I could keep from getting addicted to carrots, and after a while she started asking me about my family, you know, like if there was someone at home who was sick, who drank too much. It didn't go real well at first. I got impatient, I guess, and at one point I blurted out, "I'm tired of hearing about people who come from chemically dependent homes. My home is just fine. It's my mother who's <u>DRUNK</u> all the time: <u>That's the</u> problem."

I couldn't believe I said that, but Mrs. Nay took my hand and said that she was glad I confided in her. We talked for about 45 minutes. She told me some ways I could take care of myself, and, okay, maybe I feel a little better.

# 10 Things I Can Do To Take Good Care of Myself

1. I can spend time with friends.
2. I can exercise.
3. I can stop worrying about what I can't control.
4. I can eat healthy foods.
5. I can resist any pressure to smoke or drink.
6. I can tell myself good thoughts.
7. I can find things to do that I do well, both in school and out.
8. I can write my feelings down.
9. I can try to find humor even in tough situations.
10. I can talk with adults I trust, and ask for help when I need it.

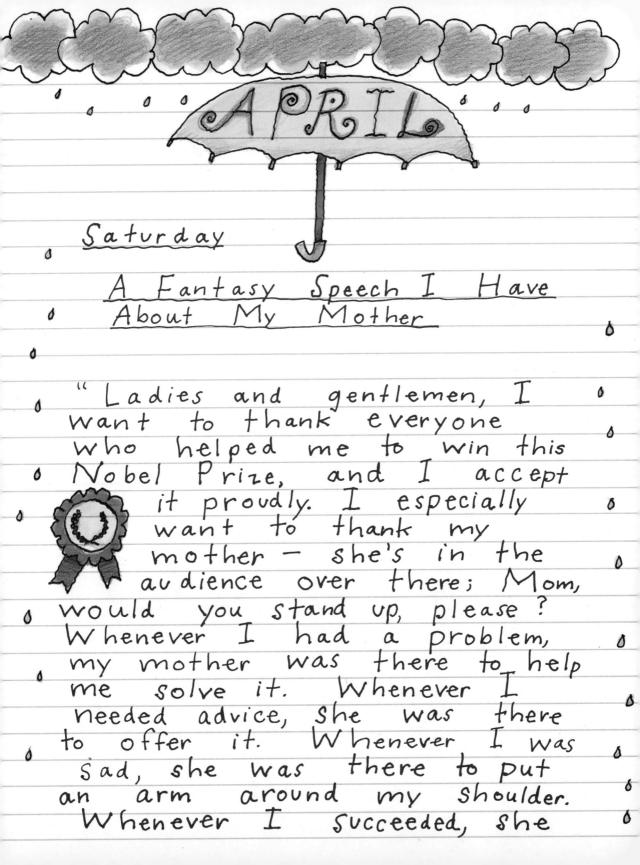

# APRIL

Saturday

## A Fantasy Speech I Have About My Mother

"Ladies and gentlemen, I want to thank everyone who helped me to win this Nobel Prize, and I accept it proudly. I especially want to thank my mother — she's in the audience over there; Mom, would you stand up, please? Whenever I had a problem, my mother was there to help me solve it. Whenever I needed advice, she was there to offer it. Whenever I was sad, she was there to put an arm around my shoulder. Whenever I succeeded, she

was there to share my
triumph. Mom, I couldn't
have won this Nobel Prize
without your support, your
guidance, and your love. I
dedicate it to you."

Monday

Today Mrs. Nay said that
I seemed to have trouble
trusting people, but I don't
know if I believe her.
    That was a joke. Ha Ha I'm
trying to be light. It's going
to take some practice.

Thursday

I flunked a spelling test today. It's because I couldn't study last night. I couldn't study last night because I couldn't keep my mind on the spelling words.

So I made up a test I can pass (I got some help from Mrs. Nay):

### A TEST

1. What can my mother do to help herself?
   a) She can admit she has a problem.
   b) She can ask for support from her family and friends.
   c) She can get help from

# A TEST
## (continued)

a counselor or other professional.

2. What can my family do to help themselves?

    a) They can admit that my mother has a problem with alcohol.

    b) They can stop protecting my mother.

    c) They can get help from a counselor or other professional.

3. What's going to happen to my mother?

    a) She may get better.

    b) She may get worse.

    c) She may stay the same.

4. What's going to happen to me?

    a) I'm going to take good care of myself.

    b) I'm going to take good care of myself.

    c) I'm going to take good care of myself.

I got 100%!!!

How to score: All the answers are correct!

<u>Saturday</u>

　　Mom got in an accident today. Drunk behind the wheel. She ran into a telephone pole. Luckily, she was only driving about ⑦ miles per hour. But she got bruised, and got into trouble with the police.

Tonight there was a big family fight, and Dad told Mom this couldn't go on and she needed to <u>"see someone"</u>. And then my brother Mark said maybe that wasn't such a bad idea, and my mother

yelled at him, and then I told Mark not to mind her because she was probably still drunk and then there was all kinds of yelling by everyone. Mom said that she didn't need any help and that we were all turning against her.

Sometimes I feel torn. It's like, she's my mother. She can't help herself. Even when she's screaming at me, I still feel that I should just accept it, because she's my mother.

<u>Monday</u>

My teacher said that she understands why I yelled at her a few months ago, and that she hopes it won't happen again, but if it does, I can always talk to her. I said, okay, thanks.

## Wednesday

Mom is in <u>treatment</u>. She agreed to go because she said she was losing too much weight and it's not healthy for her. Fine — whatever it takes. I'm not going to get excited about it. It's hard to let myself think that things could get better.

One thing, though: we're all going to a counselor now — me, Mark, Mom, and Dad. Once every two weeks. We're supposed to talk about how we "<u>function</u>" as a family, I guess. It'd be easier talking about how we <u>don't "function"</u> as a family.

Maybe it's the same thing.

## June

<u>Friday</u>

Today my mother went back into treatment. She "<u>fell off the wagon</u>." That's what my father said. Dad was doing pretty good this month — paying more attention to everyone, not clearing his throat a lot, which he does when he's nervous. I thought the whole family would fall apart when Mom fell apart. But we're actually doing okay. The sessions with the counselor are pretty interesting. The counselor said I had some good ideas, and everybody agreed. We even attended a few meetings with other families like ours, you know, where someone was an alcoholic.

Mark has had a lot of free time on his hands since he hasn't had to take care of us as much. Maybe I can find him somebody else's alcoholic parent he can look after. Just kidding! Ha Ha

. . . . . . . . . . . . . . . . . . . . . -

Tuesday

A Poem for My Mother

When you leave me, you're still here.
The screams stick to the walls
like words to a book I
have to read.
But I have read books that
frightened me
which I love.

## Wednesday

I've become pretty casual about all this. This morning I even went out of my way to tell someone that my mother was in treatment for alcoholism. He got a little quiet after that, but I thought, <u>so what.</u>

Mrs. Nay says that I've come a long way.

← forgotten tape

<u>Monday</u>

I had a fight with Susan today. She got real mad because I forgot to bring her this tape she wanted to play for her cousin who's visiting her from another state and is leaving tomorrow. It went something like this:

<u>Susan</u>: You knew how important that tape was for me!

<u>Me</u>: I'm sorry. I forgot.
<u>Susan</u>: But I'm your friend! You don't just forget something important like that with your friend!
<u>Me</u>: What do you want me to do? I said I was sorry. I'm sorry, I'm sorry, I'M SORRY!
<u>Susan</u>: You're just irresponsible,

that's all! Irresponsible and inconsiderate! I can't count on you for anything! All I ask is for you to bring me one tape, and you _can't_ even do _that_!!!

I couldn't do anything. I couldn't make her not mad, and I couldn't make myself feel less bad. I couldn't hit her, and I couldn't run away. I couldn't do _anything_. I started to cry. And she looked surprised, and then she put her arm around my shoulder. She said she was sorry she yelled at me, but she was angry. She said she would get over it and told me she was still my friend.

This is all pretty new to me.

Me    Susan

## Tuesday

Today at lunch Susan gave me a present in a box. When I opened it and removed the wax paper, I laughed. It was a _carrot_.

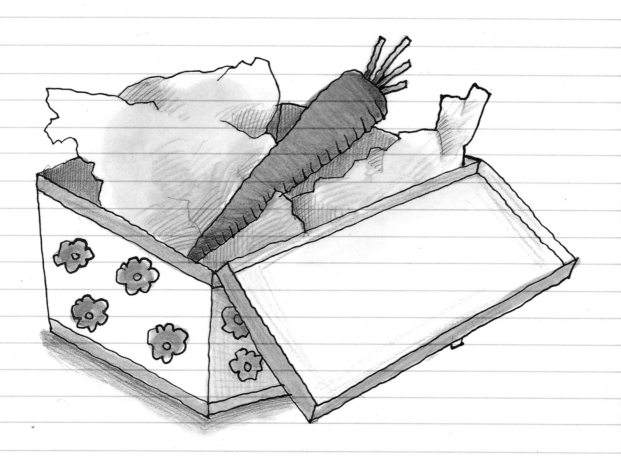

## Thursday

Mom's back home again, and she's really trying. Things are still a little awkward, but that's okay. It's better than before. We all still see the counselor, and that's okay, too. The main thing is, we're better. And I'm better, too.

I'm better because I told the forever secret.

written by  Neal Starkman

illustrated  by  Brian Karas

# Health Education Titles from
## Comprehensive Health Education Foundation

**The Apple**
by Neal Starkman
the story of a teenager's two-year decline into
alcoholism, from his first drink to his decision
to get help, told in reverse chronological order
- *recommended for teenagers*
- *included in the drug education curriculum*
  Here's Looking At You, 2000®

**Becoming Male & Female**
by Evelyn E. Ames and Lucille Trucano
a book that helps young adults understand and
accept their sexuality as a healthy, normal part
of who they are
- *recommended for teenagers and health
  education teachers*

**The Boy and the Hat**
by Neal Starkman
a story in which a strange hat serves as
a metaphor for marijuana to illustrate the
harmful effects of this drug
- *recommended for children*
- *included in the drug education curriculum*
  Here's Looking At You, 2000®

**Don't Read This Book**
by Neal Starkman
a book that challenges readers to become more
aware of themselves, to "think to think," and to
exercise independent judgement
- *recommended for teenagers*
- *included in the drug education curriculum*
  Here's Looking At You, 2000®

**Face to Face**
by Neal Starkman
a story about a teenage boy and girl who
must decide whether or not to have sex and
independently conclude that abstinence is
the best choice for them
- *recommended for teenagers*
- *included in the AIDS prevention curriculum*
  Get Real about AIDS™

**The Forever Secret**
by Neal Starkman
a journal of how a young person's experiences
with family, friends, and school are affected by
an alcoholic mother
- *recommended for children*
- *included in the drug education curriculum*
  Here's Looking At You, 2000®

**Martin the Cavebine**
by Sara Nickerson
a story that provides young children with an
understanding and appreciation of how people
are unique and worthy of consideration
- *recommended for children*
- *included in the drug education curriculum*
  Here's Looking At You, 2000®

**Miraculous Me**
by Carl Nickerson, Cheryl Smith, and
Elaine Porter-Cole
a workbook of over 100 classroom-tested games,
puzzles, and other exciting activities designed to
promote self-esteem in children
- *recommended for adults who work with
  children*

**Personal Views**
by Neal Starkman
an entertaining tale about a group of teenagers who
learn what happens when they judge people based
on labels instead of considering the whole person
- *recommended for teenagers*
- *included in the peer helping program*
  Natural Helpers®

**Peter Parrot, Private Eye**
by Sara Nickerson
the story of what Peter Parrot discovers when he
investigates why people drink, what alcohol does
to the body, and why children should never drink
alcohol
- *recommended for children*
- *included in the drug education curriculum*
  Here's Looking At You, 2000®

### Preparing for the Drug (Free) Years: A Family Activity Book

a book that provides families with information and practical skills to help prevent their children from getting involved with drugs

- *recommended for parents of children in grades 4 through 7*

### The Quitters

by Neal Starkman

a story about three friends who learn about the dangers of sidestream smoke and experience different degrees success in attempting to get their family members to stop smoking

- *recommended for children*
- *included in the drug education curriculum Here's Looking At You, 2000®*

### The Riddle

by Neal Starkman

the story about how a girl and boy become friends without even knowing it as they spend time together solving a riddle

- *recommended for children*
- *included in the drug education curriculum Here's Looking At You, 2000®*

### The Roller Coaster: A Story of Alcoholism and the Family

by Don Fitzmahan

a story that helps children in alcoholic families learn about their feelings and how to express them

- *recommended for children*
- *included in the drug education curriculum Here's Looking At You, 2000®*

### Your Decision

by Neal Starkman

a choose-your-own-ending book in which readers make decisions about relationships, drugs, and sex and then explore the consequences of those decisions

- *recommended for teenagers*
- *included in the AIDS prevention curriculum Get Real about AIDS™*

### Z's Gift

by Neal Starkman

the story of how a young boy responds to the news that his teacher has AIDS, and how he teaches adults the meaning of compassion

- *recommended for children*
- *included in the AIDS prevention curriculum Get Real about AIDS™*

## Large-Format Flip Books

*(designed for reading aloud to a group of children)*

### A Girl Named Cherie

by Neal Starkman

a series of limericks describing what happens when a young girl tries alcohol for the first time

- *recommended for adults who work with children*
- *included in the drug education curriculum Here's Looking At You, 2000®*

### Max and the House Full of Poison

by Neal Starkman

a story about how Frog teaches his friend Max, a colorful blue gorilla, how a home can be poison-proofed for young children

- *recommended for adults who work with children*
- *included in the drug education curriculum Here's Looking At You, 2000®*

### The Roller Coaster: A Story of Alcoholism and the Family

by Don Fitzmahan

a story that helps children in alcoholic families learn about their feelings and how to express them

- *recommended for adults who work with children*
- *included in the drug education curriculum Here's Looking At You, 2000®*

To order or to get more information, contact:
CHEF®
22323 Pacific Highway South
Seattle, Washington 98198
206-824-2907 or 1-800-323-CHEF